21st Century Skills Library

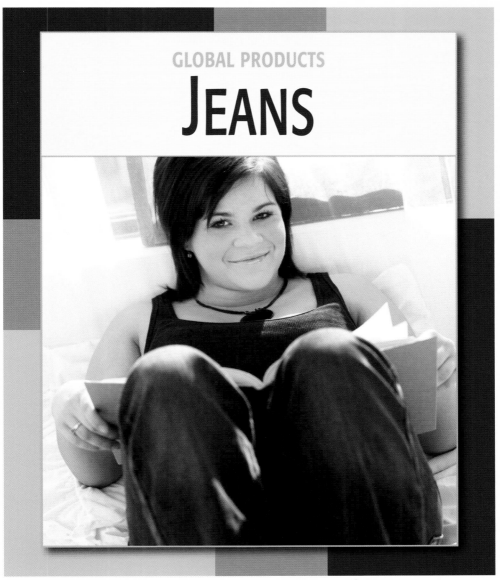
GLOBAL PRODUCTS
JEANS

Nancy Robinson Masters

Cherry Lake Publishing
Ann Arbor, Michigan

Published in the United States of America by Cherry Lake Publishing
Ann Arbor, MI
www.cherrylakepublishing.com

Content Adviser: James Sullivan, Author of *Jeans: A Cultural History of an American Icon*

Photo Credits: Pages 6 and 8, © Courtesy Levi Strauss & Co. Archives, San Francisco; page 13, © Pilar Olivares/Reuters/Corbis; page 17, © Orjan F. Ellingvag/Dagens Naringsliv/Corbis; page 19, © Viviane Moos/Corbis; page 23, © Roger Ressmeyer/Corbis; page 25, © James Marshall/Corbis

Map by XNR Productions, Inc.

Library of Congress Cataloging-in-Publication Data
Masters, Nancy Robinson.
Jeans / by Nancy Robinson Masters.
 p. cm.—(Global products)
 Includes bibliographical references.
 ISBN-13: 978-1-60279-029-2
 ISBN-10: 1-60279-029-9
1. Jeans (Clothing)—Juvenile literature. 2. Globalization—Juvenile literature. I. Title. II. Series.
TT605.M37 2008
 687'.1—dc22   2007006729

Cherry Lake Publishing would like to acknowledge the work of
The Partnership for 21st Century Skills.
Please visit www.21stcenturyskills.org for more information.

TABLE OF CONTENTS

CHAPTER ONE

A LOT TO TALK ABOUT

Jeans come in many different colors and styles.

Bzzzzzzz! Hailey Hernandez hurried to the laundry room the moment the dryer signal sounded. After she finished helping her mom sort, fold, and hang the clothes, she would be allowed to e-mail her pen pals Lin Cheng and Ravi Patel.

Hailey lives near Lubbock, Texas. Lin Cheng lives in the Yangtze River region of China. Ravi Patel lives in Punjab, India. The three fifth-graders are part of a program for students with an interest in agriculture. The program helps students to improve their communication skills while learning about life in other countries. Though they live thousands of miles apart in countries with different cultures and customs, Hailey, Lin, and Ravi have one thing in common: each lives on a farm where cotton is the main crop grown.

"Hailey, I have a surprise," Mrs. Hernandez announced as she folded the last towel. "Lin and Ravi are coming to Lubbock with their parents next month. The Lins and Patels are among hundreds of cotton growers from more than 80 countries coming here for important talks."

Hailey squealed and tossed her brother's socks into the air.

"For real, Mom? Lin and Ravi are coming to Texas? What are their parents and all of the other people coming here to talk about that is so important?"

Mrs. Hernandez laughed as she reached in the dryer and took out Hailey's favorite pair of pants.

"They're coming to talk about jeans!"

CHAPTER TWO

WHO INVENTED JEANS?

Click! Hailey's fingers stretched across the keyboard.

"Who invented jeans?" she typed to her pen pals.

"The Chinese word for jeans is *niuzaiku*," Lin Cheng e-mailed back.

*Levi Strauss was born in Germany in 1829 and
came to the United States in 1847.*

"That means 'cowboy pants.' Perhaps jeans were invented by the American cowboys we love to watch in movies."

"No, it wasn't the American cowboy who invented jeans," Ravi replied. "India was the first to export a thick cotton cloth known as *dungaree* that was used to make pants more than 300 years ago. Perhaps the inventor was from India."

"Well, my ancestors were weaving cotton even before that," Hailey wrote. "Archaeologists have found pieces of cotton cloth they believe to be more than 6,000 years old in caves in Mexico. Maybe the farmer who grew the first cotton is the one who invented jeans!"

German immigrant Levi Strauss is often credited with inventing jeans. He worked with an immigrant from Latvia, a man named Jacob Davis, to invent jeans as we know them today. Davis lived in Reno, Nevada, and made clothing for miners and other laborers during the famous California and Nevada gold rush days of the mid-1800s. He used heavy woven cotton material that he ordered from Strauss, a merchant in San Francisco.

Davis and Strauss called their product "waist overalls," the name given to men's work pants at that time. Davis came up with the idea to use copper rivets (fasteners) to strengthen the pockets when the miners complained about how easily the pockets tore. He persuaded Strauss to patent the copper pocket fastener design. Patent No. 139,121 for "Improvement in Fastening Pocket-Openings" was issued to the two men in 1873.

Levi Strauss & Company was the only company allowed to make riveted pants until the patent expired in 1890. Then dozens of garment manufacturers began to imitate the original riveted clothing made popular by Levi Strauss & Company.

The patent for riveted pants was issued to Davis and Strauss in 1873.

The first advertisement for women's jeans appeared in a magazine in 1935. Until then, most women considered jeans basic work clothing for men. By the end of World War II (1939–1945), thousands of women working in factories were wearing the jeans that their husbands, fathers, and brothers had left behind when they went to serve in the military.

Fashion history was made in the 1950s when film star James Dean and rock 'n' roll legend Elvis Presley wore jeans. By the 1960s, wearing jeans had become a fashion symbol of American pop culture.

Since the 1970s, jeans have become part of the fashions worn by men, women, teens, and children—not only in the United States, but also in other countries such as the former Soviet Union. Jeans were once forbidden there because they symbolized the American way of life, which Soviet leaders opposed.

21st Century Content

The blue in blue jeans comes from indigo dye. China, India, and Japan used indigo plants for centuries to make dye. The dye was also known to ancient civilizations in Greece, Rome, Britain, Peru, and Africa. Since the late 1800s, indigo dye has been made from chemicals, not plants. Dust-free powder now provides a better way to control air and water pollution in the fabric dyeing process.

Over the years, different treatments to the dyed-blue fabric have been introduced that give jeans their unique coloring and look. Prewashed, stonewashed, sandblasted, and vintage/ripped are the most popular. While jeans are now available in almost every color, blue is still the favorite of most consumers. More than a billion pairs of jeans have been dyed blue.

21st Century Content

In 2007, the average price for a new pair of jeans in the United States was $25. That would be about the same as:

12 United Kingdom pounds

19 euros

32 Australian dollars

35 Turkey new liras

142 Egyptian pounds

193 Chinese yuan

273 Mexican pesos

662 Russian rubles

1,100 Indian rupees

1,500 Pakistan rupees

3,000 Japanese yen

225,000 Indonesian rupiahs

Worn, torn, faded jeans can cost even more! Certain brands of jeans of any age or condition can bring more than $1,000 U.S. a pair! In countries where the value of money changes rapidly, consumers actually prefer jeans instead of cash because the value of the jeans is more stable.

By 2000, there were hundreds of brands of jeans in the world, including jeans made by apparel designers for specialty markets. Jeans can be found anywhere from exclusive shops to emergency shelters for the homeless, in almost every country in the world.

Jeans can also be found in outer space! Both American astronauts and Russian cosmonauts in the International Space Station wear jeans as they orbit Earth.

CHAPTER THREE

THE JOURNEY TO JEANS

Sports and jeans are a perfect team!

"There they are!" Hailey waved her jeans jacket in the air as Lin Cheng, Ravi Patel, and their parents stepped into the terminal at the Lubbock Preston Smith International Airport. The crowded terminal was filled with cotton growers, clothing manufacturers, and distributors arriving from around the world.

"We knew we were getting close to the High Plains of Texas when all we could see were fields of cotton under the airplane's wings," Ravi said as he shook hands with Mr. and Mrs. Hernandez. "What an amazing sight! No wonder Texas is known as the buckle of the Cotton Belt."

"Most of the farms in China are very small, sometimes only a few hectares," Lin Cheng said. She gave Mr. and Mrs. Hernandez a bow of greeting, then gave Hailey a huge hug.

"A hectare is equal to 2.5 acres," Ravi's father explained as they walked to the baggage claim area. "India has about 9 million hectares (about 20 million acres) planted in cotton, the largest acreage of any nation in the world! However, we do not produce as much cotton as China or the United States. Hailey's family can plant and harvest 2,000 acres of cotton because they have technology and equipment not available in some remote farming areas. In some developing countries, they still do all the planting and harvesting by hand or with animals instead of with machines."

"Can you believe we are wearing jeans that are exactly alike?" Lin Cheng asked Hailey. "Just think! The cotton for our jeans may have been grown on your farm here in Texas, made into denim cloth, and sent to China to be made into jeans by garment workers like my parents."

Ravi chimed in, "Your jeans may have been exported from China and imported by clothing buyers for stores in the United States or India or South America or Europe or Canada . . ." He stopped talking.

Hailey and Lin Cheng were too busy making plans to go jeans shopping to listen to him!

A boy picks cotton in Peru. Cotton is still harvested by hand in many places around the world.

The Cotton Belt describes an area including 17 states that stretch across the middle and southern half of the United States, where cotton is the main cash crop. An estimated 13 million acres (5.3 million hectares) of cotton will be planted in the Cotton Belt in 2007. These states have three main things in common: lots of sunshine, water, and fertile soil. The U.S. cotton industry accounts for more than $25 billion in products and services. Jeans are just one of the many textile products that are made from cotton. Sheets, towels, upholstery, rugs, bandages, and even U.S. paper money are made with cotton. What other items can you name?

A pair of cotton jeans begins as a seed. The seeds from wild cotton growing in Mexico—the kind that was woven by Hailey's ancestors more than 6,000 years ago—would not produce the kind of cotton needed to meet the requirements of today's jeans manufacturers. Cotton must be "processing friendly." Seeds are scientifically developed to fit not only specific climates and soil conditions, but also to produce fibers that are compatible with machinery used to spin cotton thread and weave cloth. The machinery is controlled by computer programs that are so precise, they can measure the length of a cotton fiber to 1/100th of an inch.

Bt cotton is cotton grown from genetically modified seeds. The seeds are altered so they contain bacteria. These altered seeds produce plants that

Each cotton boll contains nearly 500,000 fibers that can be spun into thread.

Do you have any idea where your jeans were made? It is likely that they were made in a factory halfway around the world and shipped to the store where you bought them.

What impact do you think the globalization of manufacturing will have on your future? What are some things you can do to help prepare yourself for living and working in a global economy?

resist crop-destroying insects called boll weevils. This helps farmers grow more cotton. Agronomists in some countries, however, believe that the land and water used to grow cotton could better be used to grow food. Governments in these countries often discourage farmers from planting Bt cotton.

Cotton is harvested with machines or by human labor, depending on where it is grown. A cotton gin then separates the fiber from the seeds and packs the fiber into bales of lint called Universal Density Bales. Each UD Bale weighs about 500 pounds (227 kilograms). A sample of fiber is taken from each bale to determine its quality. The bale of cotton is marketed to a mill, where it is made into cloth. The cloth is sold to a manufacturer that produces cotton products that are sold to consumers.

While their parents attended the cotton conference, Hailey, Lin, and Ravi toured the American Cotton Growers Mill in Littlefield, Texas, about 20 miles (32 kilometers) north of Lubbock.

Today's computer-operated cotton gins rapidly separate fibers from seeds.

21st Century Content

The first machine known to separate cottonseeds from cotton fiber was the Churka, sometimes called the Charka. It was used in India more than 3,000 years ago.

American inventor Eli Whitney perfected the "cotton engine" in 1794. Whitney's "gin" made it possible to separate seeds from fiber more quickly. This created an enormous demand for more cotton and led to major social and industrial changes around the world. Robert S. Munger developed "system ginning" in the late 1800s. This was a method for transferring cotton from the boll to the bale in one continuous process. Modern cotton gins have applied computer technology and equipment to this method to rapidly separate fiber from seeds.

"My grandfather and other cotton farmers on the High Plains decided in 1976 not only to grow cotton, but also to make denim right here with the cotton they grew," said Hailey. "They formed the world's only farmer-owned denim manufacturing plant. From three million to five million bales of cotton are made into denim here each year. What's picked in the field one day can be material for jeans the next!"

Lin and Ravi watched as baled cotton was separated into small tufts and then blended with various cotton fibers. From there, they saw the fibers spun, woven, dyed, finished, packed, and readied for shipment to garment manufacturers.

What an amazing sight!

CHAPTER FOUR

LET'S TRADE!

Lin Cheng zipped up the jeans she was trying on and whirled around to look at the back pockets in the mirror of the shopping mall dressing room.

Workers in a Chinese factory use sewing machines to make denim jeans.

"Ooooh, those jeans are so cool," Hailey said. "All my friends are wearing them."

"These jeans were made in China at the factory where my mother works," Lin said proudly.

"Girls in India wear those same jeans!" Ravi said when Lin Cheng came out of the dressing room.

Countries in Europe, Asia, South America, and Australia are growing more cotton and producing their own denim to manufacture jeans. This has increased global competition among manufacturers and made jeans more affordable in some countries. It has also increased costs in other countries and created new trade challenges.

For example, countries use tariffs and quotas to control the number of foreign products that can be imported into a country or exported to another country. A tariff is a tax placed on goods from another country. A quota is a limitation on the number of items that may be brought in.

When quotas were removed on shipments of jeans to the United States in 2003, China flooded the United States with four times as many jeans in 2005 as they had shipped in 2004. While this was good for China, it was bad for other countries that could not produce enough jeans to compete with China in the U.S. market.

Imports without tariffs and quotas have also made it difficult for U.S. jeans manufacturers to compete in the marketplace. Government regulations involving the "3 Ws"—wages, working conditions, and waste management—differ from country to country. Each of these factors plays an important role in determining the price and quality of jeans.

Although textile manufacturing in the United States has decreased, U.S.-made jeans are in high demand all over the world. Labels on jeans identify the country where the jeans are made. This allows consumers to choose which country's jeans they wish to buy in addition to choosing the quality, price, and fit.

21st Century Content

Where are the jeans made that are imported into the United States? According to the U.S. Department of Commerce, if 100 pairs of jeans represented all the jeans that were imported in 2006:

43 pairs were made in Mexico

8 pairs were made in Hong Kong

6 pairs were made in China

5 pairs were made in Guatemala

3 pairs were made in Cambodia

3 pairs were made in Colombia

2 pairs were made in Bangladesh

2 pairs were made in Lesotho

2 pairs were made in Costa Rica

2 pairswere made in the Philippines

2 pairs were made in Nicaragua

The remaining pairs represent all the jeans that are manufactured elsewhere in the world combined.

How are jeans made? Some jeans are cut and sewn by hand. One or two individuals may make each pair from start to finish, and each pair is unique. Other jeans are made by assembly-line workers in factories. Let's visit a jeans factory in Thailand that produces 2,500 pairs a day, to discover how it is done:

First, a pattern maker draws a jeans pattern. It takes about 15 pieces to make a standard pattern for a pair of five-pocket jeans.

Next, a computer will create a "puzzle" outline of the pieces on paper. The puzzle outline is placed on top of the denim. Up to a hundred layers of denim are laid out on a cutting table. A cutting machine cuts along the puzzle outline and the pieces of cut denim are put into bundles marked with the jeans size they are to be used for.

Workers at machines sew the pieces together. It takes about 15 minutes to sew a pair of jeans together from the cut pieces.

The jeans then go to a jeans washing plant. Stonewashed jeans are washed with smooth pumice stones in water for up to six hours to produce different shades and patterns.

Each pair of jeans is made up of a number of pieces,
such as these leg pieces, cut from a pattern.

After washing, the jeans are inspected for damage or flaws. Buttons and rivets are placed using a special type of press before the jeans go to the garment packing room. Another quality check is made before the labels are added to each pair.

The last step is packing the jeans for shipment in boxes, bags, or bundles. How jeans are packed for shipping depends on the requirements of the country where they are to be shipped.

Transporting jeans from the factory to the customer often takes more time than actually manufacturing the jeans. It took a week for the jeans Lin Cheng's mother helped make to travel by truck from the factory to the shipping dock in China. The boxes were placed in a special sea container, which holds between 9,500 and 11,000 pairs of jeans. They spent six weeks on the ship before arriving at the Port of Houston. An international freight broker handled the customs requirements. Five days later, a truck delivered the jeans to the store in Lubbock where Hailey and Lin were shopping.

"I'll take this pair," Lin told the sales clerk. "I want my friends to know I bought a pair of jeans in Texas that were made in China."

CHAPTER FIVE

THE JEANS TEAM
OF THE FUTURE

*Jeans are among the popular items for sale
at this outdoor market in Lagos, Nigeria.*

"Take good care of my jeans, and I'll take good care of yours."

Hailey's voice could hardly be heard over the crowd at the security area of Lubbock's airport, where her friends were standing in line. The three friends had given each other a pair of their favorite jeans to remind them of their time together in the Cotton Belt of Texas.

"We're going to trade back when we meet next year at the cotton conference in India," Hailey explained to her mother as they headed back to the airport's parking lot.

∾

Jeans will be an even bigger part of the global economy by the time the three friends see each other again. It is likely that more aircraft will be used to speed the delivery of jeans and other products between countries. A Boeing 767 cargo jet can fly 3,000 miles (4,828 km) carrying 132,000 pounds (59,874 kg) of jeans without having to land to refuel!

This will mean more highways, bigger bridges, and better roads will be needed in many countries to transport the jeans to consumers after they arrive at an airport or by ship. Building these highways, bridges, and roads will mean more jobs. More jobs will mean workers will have more money to buy more jeans!

The jeans team of the future will include accountants, box makers, carpenters, designers, environmental engineers, farmers, garment inspectors, health care workers, inventors, judges, keyboard operators, logistics experts, mechanics, needle makers, office workers, pilots, quality assurance inspectors, rail transportation workers, sewing machine operators, tailors, upholsterers, vocational education teachers, welders, x-ray technicians, yarn dyers, and even zookeepers who wear jeans!

Many workers, such as this carpenter, wear jeans because they are comfortable and the denim fabric is strong.

Learning & Innovation Skills

Why do you think kids all over the world agree that jeans are one of their favorite things to wear? Think about why you like to wear jeans. Here are some ideas to get you started:

- Jeans are comfortable.
- Jeans have pockets.
- It is okay to get jeans dirty!
- Jeans can be cute, casual, or dressy.
- Jeans are always in style. They match everything!

These are just a few of the hundreds of jeans-related careers for which more workers will be needed. Most of all, the jeans team of the future will need friends such as Hailey Hernandez, Ravi Patel, and Lin Cheng working together to build a better world for everyone.

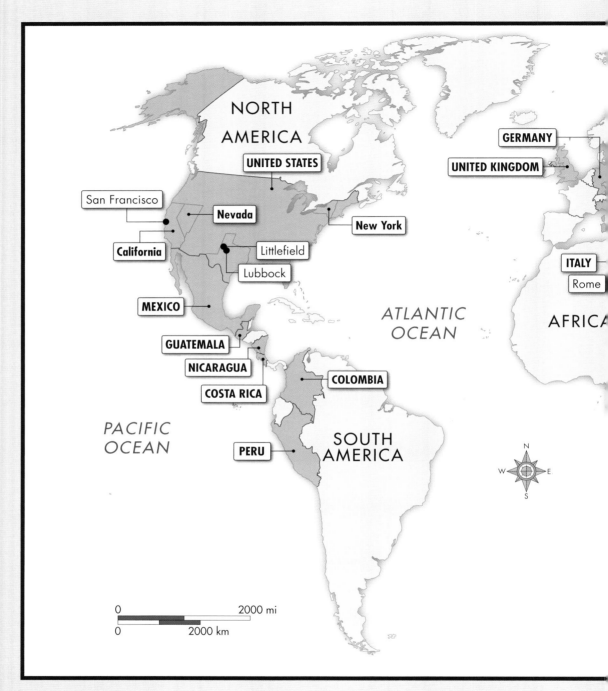

NORTH
AMERICA

UNITED STATES

San Francisco

Nevada

California

Littlefield

Lubbock

New York

MEXICO

GUATEMALA

NICARAGUA

COSTA RICA

COLOMBIA

PERU

SOUTH
AMERICA

PACIFIC
OCEAN

ATLANTIC
OCEAN

GERMANY

UNITED KINGDOM

ITALY

Rome

AFRICA

N
W E
S

0   2000 mi

0   2000 km

This map shows the countries and cities mentioned in the text.

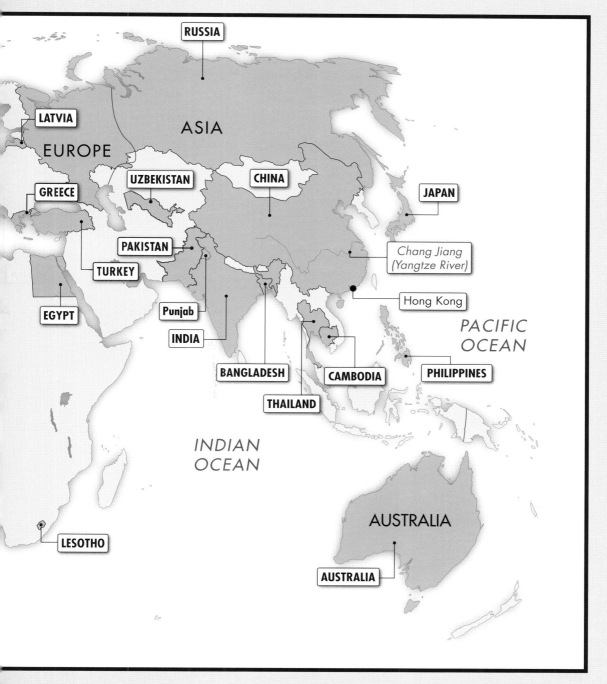

RUSSIA

LATVIA

EUROPE

ASIA

GREECE

UZBEKISTAN

CHINA

JAPAN

PAKISTAN

TURKEY

Chang Jiang (Yangtze River)

EGYPT

Punjab

Hong Kong

PACIFIC OCEAN

INDIA

BANGLADESH

CAMBODIA

PHILIPPINES

THAILAND

INDIAN OCEAN

AUSTRALIA

LESOTHO

AUSTRALIA

They are the locations of some of the companies involved in the making and selling of jeans.

Glossary

agronomists (uh-GROH-nuh-mists) scientists who study crop production and soil management

Bt cotton (BEE-TEE KOT-uhn) cotton grown from genetically modified seeds that contain bacteria that make the plants resistant to boll weevils

customs (KUS-tums) a payment that must be made to a country's government when importing goods to that country

exported (ek-SPORT-ed) sent (as in products) to another country to be sold there

imported (im-PORT-ed) brought into a country for sale or trade

logistics (luh-JIS-tiks) the handling of the details of obtaining, maintaining, and transporting materials and products

patent (PAT-uhnt) to obtain the legal document giving an inventor the sole rights to manufacture and sell his or her invention

sandblasted (SAND-blas-ted) fabric that is sprayed with tiny grains of sand or hand-rubbed with sandpaper to lighten the color and soften the feel

stonewashed (STONE-washd) washed with pumice stone to soften (as in fabric) and give it a worn look

textile (TEK-stile) cloth or fabric that has been woven or knitted

vintage (VIN-tij) fabric that is made to look old and worn, sometimes by cutting or tearing

waste management (WASTE MAN-ij-ment) reducing damage to the environment from waste

FOR MORE INFORMATION

Books

Kyi, Tanya Lloyd. *The Blue Jean Book: The Story Behind the Seams*. Toronto: Annick Press, 2005.

Masters, Nancy Robinson. *The Cotton Gin: Inventions That Shaped the World*. New York: Franklin Watts, 2006.

Web Sites

Artists Helping Children: Blue Jeans Arts and Crafts for Kids
artistshelpingchildren.org/bluejeansartscraftsideasprojectskids.html
Creative ideas for decorating denim and craft making with jeans

National Cotton Council of America: The Story of Cotton
www.cotton.org/pubs/cottoncounts/story/pdf.cfm
Tells the story of where and how cotton is grown, processed, and woven into cloth

INDEX

ABOUT THE AUTHOR

Nancy Robinson Masters has been wearing jeans all of her life. Nancy grew up on a cotton farm in West Texas where she learned to drive a tractor before she learned to drive a car. She is an award-winning author of 18 books and hundreds of stories and articles.

"That old tractor started me on journeys that have taken me around the world. Everywhere I've been, including Antarctica as a guest of the National Science Foundation, I've met people wearing jeans!"